AN UNFAITHFUL LOVE

By Danielle McGee

Contents

Chapter 1

Damn. Why me? Was it not bad enough that my mother neglected me pretty much my whole life? That she never gave me words of encouragement or told me I was beautiful? That she did the unthinkable to me? Let me take you back a little to tell you how it all started.

It was May of 2015, and I had just graduated with a major in accounting. I was so anxious for my life to begin—to get the dream job I'd been hoping for. I decided to stay in Texas because the opportunities were greater, and moving back to Tennessee just wasn't an option for me. But I was in for a rude awakening. Every interviewer turned me down because I didn't have any experience. So, for the time being, I had to make due as a customer service rep at a cable company. My friend Kelsie helped me get the job, which paid $13.50 an hour. I couldn't afford an apartment at the time, so until I saved enough money, I was stuck staying an extended stay.

I started feeling so stagnated. I had the same old routines. Go to Rickey's coffee shop after work, have tacos on Tuesday with Kelsie, apply for internships, and binge-watch shows on the weekends. That went on for months until one day, during my break at work, I received a text. It was Lamar, my best friend from high school. He told me he had just moved to the area and would like to see me so we could catch up. We met at Rickey's coffee shop after I got off that evening. When I saw him, I ran up and gave him the tightest hug. We both stood there looking at one another, grinning from ear to ear. We got our drinks and went out to the patio, where I asked him what made him want to move to Texas.

He said, "I was contacted by a contractor working at the chemical plant, and I couldn't turn down what he was offering."

That was understandable; Lamar had always been a go-getter. We stayed at the coffee shop, laughing and talking until they were getting ready to close. He walked me to my car and hugged me; then we went on our way.

* * *

Once I got home and settled, Lamar called me to make sure I made it back safely. I replied, "Yes," very sarcastically. We laughed, and then he asked me if I'd like to hang out again on the weekend. I wasn't doing anything important, plus, I was thrilled to have my best friend in the same city with me again, so I said, "Sure" without hesitation, and we decided on Saturday at 6:00 p.m. Then we said our goodnights and got off the phone.

As I finished up my week at work, Kelsie and I went to a few clothing stores before it was time for me to meet up with Lamar. He texted me and asked what I was in the mood to do, but I wasn't sure, so I suggested we meet at a restaurant that had really good seafood. That way, we could think of something together. I finished shopping with Kelsie, and I went back home to get dressed. When I made it to the restaurant, Lamar was already there, sitting in his mustang with the roof back, trying to look cool. He walked over to my car and asked if I wanted to get the food to go so that we could head back to his apartment. He wanted to hang out so we could talk without being rushed before things closed.

"I wish you would have told me before I got overdressed," I said.

He chuckled and said, "Aww, you'll be alright. I got some shorts you can put on." Once we got our food, I followed him back to his place, where we talked and laughed about the old days. We had so many memories together, we could have gone on forever. As it got later, he asked me if I'd like a glass of Hennessey.

I said, "Sure. Cognac is still my favorite liquor," and he chuckled, replying, "Mine too."

He put on some old-school '90s music, and we just vibed, listening to different songs. He asked me why I never gave him a chance in school. I was shocked that he even asked me that. "Because we were always just friends," I said. "Besides, you had a girlfriend at the time."

He said, "Yeah, but what if I told you I've been in love with you since high school?"

I coughed up some of my drink when he said that. I needed a moment to go clean up the drink I'd spilled on my blouse—and to gather my thoughts. When I came out of the bathroom, Lamar was in the kitchen making himself another drink. He apologized for making me feel uncomfortable, but the mood still felt kind of awkward after that. I decided to just leave so that I could have some time to process what Lamar had said to me, but I wouldn't have a chance to do that. As I walked towards the door, keys in hand, Lamar came in from behind, turned me around, and gently grabbed me, pulling me closer to him. I started to feel tingling through my body as he took my face in his hands. "You're the woman I want to be with," he said, kissing me softly. Then he picked me up and took me to his room. Slowly laying me on his bed, he pulled off my clothes and started eating me like a banana cream pie. Hearing my moans, he came up and kissed my lips as he entered me, slowly stroking me all the while, gazing into my eyes and whispering sweet things in my ear. Lamar and I made love three times that night. Later, we took a shower together, and he held me until we fell asleep.

The next morning, he woke me up with my favorite: a caramel Frappuccino. We sat up all morning, cuddling, and talking about our goals and giving each other affirmations. I had never seen that side of him before. He was so affectionate and open about his thoughts.

Later that afternoon, my job called me to see if I could work the following day for a few hours. I wanted to decline, but I was saving to get my own place, so I looked at Lamar sadly and said I had to get going. I gathered my things, and then he walked me downstairs and gave me a hug and a kiss.

On my way home, I was still in disbelief. I really hadn't seen it coming, but it felt good to have that butterfly feeling again. The last time I had felt like that was with my ex—the one who'd taken my virginity during my first year of college.

After I got home, I called Lamar to let him know I'd made it safely, and then I settled down and filled out some more intern applications. Another week was soon to start.

Chapter 2

The next day at work, Kelsie and I had the same shift. She was kind of nosey; the first question she asked was how things with Lamar had gone. "What did y'all end up doing?" I started getting flashbacks of how Lamar had caressed my body and made love to me when she asked that, but I wasn't ready to tell anyone about us yet, so I laughed it off, switching the subject.

Lamar and I texted throughout my whole shift. It sounded like gibberish when Kelsie kept talking about her recent date with some guy named Andre she'd met on the Internet. I was already getting used to Lamar calling once I got home from work. He was so protective of me, and I liked it; it was the opposite feeling I'd experienced as a child.

Weeks went by, and we became inseparable. Since Lamar and I were now serious, I was ready to introduce Kelsie to him, so we met up that Saturday night at a lounge called TJ's. She also brought along her friend Andre. We introduced ourselves to each other, ordered some drinks, and mingled. As it got later, Kelsie said she had to make an announcement.

"Andre and I are moving to California," she said, waving surprise hands in the air. In total shock, I asked her when she was leaving, and she said, "In two weeks."

I asked her to walk over to the bar with me. The music was loud, so I leaned in, saying, "You hardly know him. Why are you moving?"

"Because I love him, Alexis, and he just got a great job making six figures a year." It didn't make sense to me, but who was I to say anything? I was in love, too. I wasn't in the mood to mingle anymore after Kelsie gave me the news that she was moving, so Lamar and I said our goodnights and left.

That Monday, when I got to work, my manager called me into his office. I didn't know what to expect because he always had a straight face. He said, "I've been informed that Kelsie is resigning from the company, and we need a new team lead. Since she's leaving, would you be interested in taking that position?"

My eyes lit up. "Yes, sir," I said.

"Good deal," he replied. "I'll have Kelsie train you before she leaves."

* * *

I dreaded those two weeks, knowing my friend wasn't going to be living in the same city as me anymore. I decided to throw them a moving away party at TJ's the night before Kelsie and Andre left. I invited a few of our associates from college. I tried my best to interact with everyone, but Kelsie leaving really bothered me. I guess she could see it in my face because she walked over with two shots of cognac in her hand, telling me to cheer up. She was right, so I stopped acting like a party pooper and put my feelings aside. We didn't leave the lounge that morning until 2:00 a.m. All of us got tipsy, but Lamar and I still managed to meet back up with them later that morning before they left for their flight. We still looked a mess, with hardly any sleep and bags under our eyes, but I had to see her off and get some last-minute hugs in because I knew it would be a while before we'd see each other again. Afterward, Lamar and I went back to his apartment to sleep.

Later that evening, he woke me by rubbing on my thighs, kissing my neck, and slightly shaking me. "Huh?" I responded, my voice still scratchy.

"I want to ask you something."

"What is it?" I asked.

"Will you move in with me?"

I lay there in silence, stunned by the question but eventually asking him to let me think about it because I had finally saved enough money to get my own apartment. I may as well have said yes, though, because I started staying over at his place almost every night. I even had my own dresser full of clothes.

* * *

Everything was going great two weeks after officially moving in with him. I was finally selected for the accounting internship at a corporate office. I would only have four months to do, and then I would become a full-time accountant, starting off at forty-eight thousand a year. I was still working my other job, too, so things were finally looking up for me.

Chapter 3

For about two months, everything was going great with my internship. What was more, Lamar and I had our first Christmas and New Year's together as a couple. Everything was going great . . . until I missed my period. I didn't want to tell Lamar right away—not until I was sure—so I called off work the next day to see the doctor.

Lo and behold, I was six weeks pregnant. It didn't surprise me much because we made love every chance we got. It would often be intense, so he didn't always wear protection. I was so upset with myself that I hadn't taken better precautions, and I still had two months left in the internship program. Since Valentine's day was right around the corner, I thought giving him the results as a gift would be perfect. He had booked us a small getaway that weekend at a resort. He surprised me with a candlelit dinner, and afterward we headed over to the Jacuzzi. He dimmed the lights and turned on some R&B. As we conversed and enjoyed the mood, I grabbed his hand and placed it on my stomach.

He chuckled and said, "Baby, what made you do that?"

I took a deep breath. I was nervous, not knowing how he was going to take the news. At last, I said, "I'm pregnant."

He looked zoned out for about a minute. Then he grinned and started talking to my belly and thinking of crazy baby names.

* * *

A few weeks into finding out about the pregnancy, I started feeling fatigued and nauseous most of the time. It had begun to affect my attendance and job performance. I called in sick to both jobs at least two days a week; I could only miss seven days of the internship before they dropped me from the program. I tried explaining my situation to the program director, but she wasn't understanding at all.

She said, "You only get one more time before you're dropped."

That same week, I resigned from the cable company to focus strictly on the internship, but it was pointless. Two weeks into finally getting back on track with everything, the director decided to pull some excuse to drop me from the program because I was thirty minutes late to a supposedly very important mandatory meeting.

At home, I sobbed into Lamar's shoulder as he tried to comfort me. Just like that, I was back to square one with nothing to show for all the hard work I had put in over those past months. I tried getting my job back at the cable company, but they had already filled my position. I already knew filling out more intern applications was a waste of time because it had taken so long for me to get employed in the first place.

Weeks went by, and there I was, feeling sorry for myself. My birthday was right around the corner, so Kelsie said she would come down to celebrate with me. At this point, I found out I would be having twins, so that brought some excitement back to my life. At 1:00 p.m., on the Saturday before my birthday, I received a call from Kelsie's mom. She said Kelsie had been beaten to death by Andre. I was lost for words because I had just talked to her about coming down for my birthday. After the call ended, I stood there with the phone still to my ear, hoping I was dreaming. But I wasn't. Her mom called me back early in the week to discuss the funeral arrangements.

A day before my birthday, I watched them lower my friend into the ground, bawling my eyes out, thinking about our college days, going shopping together, and our favorite: Taco Tuesdays. As it turned out, Andre had confessed to the police. Evidently, he had a terrible temper, and when he found out she was coming to see her family and me, he'd feared she wouldn't come back, so he took her life.

I spent the rest of the afternoon consoling her family and reminiscing about the good times. That evening, after making it home, I couldn't even think of what I wanted to do for my birthday. I went to bed sobbing, and Lamar soothed me to sleep. On April 10, my birthday, Lamar woke me with my favorite caramel Frappuccino, scrambled eggs, and turkey bacon. "Happy twenty-fourth," he said. "Get excited because I have a surprise for you."

Once we dressed, he blindfolded and guided me to the car. When we made it to the mysterious location, he guided me up a staircase that felt never-ending. He started a guessing game for me to think about where we could be. After I guessed wrong a few times, he finally took the blindfold off.

It was a beautiful big house. I said, "Baby, what made you want to rent an Airbnb?"

He chuckled and said, "This is our house."

"When did you plan all this?" I asked.

"I've been saving for a while," he said. "When you were at your internship and work, I would meet with the realtor. Do you like it?"

"Of course!" I said.

He grabbed my hand and opened the door. I was as excited as a kid at an adventure park. I couldn't wait to see our new house, and once we got a few steps in, all I heard was, "Surprise!" Lamar had invited our friends and family from Tennessee. I was so surprised and overwhelmed with joy to see everyone.

Lamar said he had sent the invitations weeks ago. Kelsie's passing had been so unexpected that it had made him want to cheer me up even more. While Lamar and I had our fond moment together, someone tapped me on the shoulder. It was my mom, Lisa. It was the first time I'd seen her since I had left for college. She embraced me with the tightest hug and gave me the biggest smile I could remember coming from her. "How did you get down here?" I asked.

She said, "Your uncle Troy brought me." I immediately started scanning the room, looking for him, and when I spotted him, all I could see was his one gold tooth shining and his button-down shirt and black slacks. We embraced each other immediately. He'd always been my favorite uncle, and he'd taken me in during my last year of high school, so he was astonished on how far I had come.

After I greeted everyone and mingled for a while, Lamar came out to the patio. Interrupting everyone, he walked over to me, grabbed my hand, and said, "I have one more surprise for you." He started giving an emotional speech that had me bawling my eyes out. I couldn't believe it—that someone could love me that much and actually show it. He got down on one knee and asked me to marry him. I said yes, and everyone clapped and cheered for us. I felt like I was on cloud nine. The evening couldn't have been any better.

Later that night, before everyone left to go to their hotels, my mother pulled me aside. She asked me if I could meet up with her the next morning before they left so we could talk about something that had been on her mind.

The following morning, everyone met us for breakfast. My mother seemed kind of annoyed because she had just wanted it to be us, but since everyone was getting on the road around the same time, they thought it would be better just to leave from the restaurant. I was still curious about what it was that my mom wanted to talk to me about, so we got a separate table on the other side of the restaurant to make her more comfortable. She sat there, staring at me for the longest time before she finally said that she was proud of me. The energy was a little weird at first until we started warming up to each other. She apologized for putting her needs and men before me while I was growing up. She begged me to forgive her for not being there like she should have. She said having me at fifteen hadn't been easy, and that she wasn't ready to be a parent at the time. Then she said, "The reason I asked you to breakfast is that I want to start over with you. I would like to move here for a little while and help you with the twins when they get here." My eyes stretched wide after she asked that, not knowing at that moment whether to tell her to kick rocks or give her a date to move in. I didn't want to be selfish and withhold my kids from having a grandmother because of our history, though, so I asked her to give me some time to talk it over with Lamar.

After we finished breakfast and saw everyone off, Lamar and I headed back to the apartment to start packing. It took a few weeks for us to finally get the house the way we wanted it, but it was worth it. In the process, we found out we were having boys—exactly what we had prayed for, so that was even more exciting.

Chapter 4

We decided to let my mother come live with us for a little while before the boys arrived, and I was glad we did. At thirty-seven weeks, I had to have an emergency C-section because one of the babies was in distress. It was one of the longest and scariest hours I had ever experienced, but I had captured another memorable moment. Lamar Jr. was six pounds three ounces, and Jackson was five pounds four ounces. After a few days in the hospital, we got the green light to be discharged.

The next day, Lamar had to get back to work. Although it didn't leave him much bonding time with the boys, the bills still had to be paid, so I was grateful to have my mother helping me attend to the boys since I could hardly move around. In the midst of everything, she was trying to make up for lost time, so she asked me a lot of questions. Most answers she'd have known if she had spent any time with me over the years, but I was ready to leave the past in the past and start fresh so that I could be the best role model for my kids.

After a few weeks of healing, I was back on my feet, and we formulated a schedule: I would watch the boys through the day, and my mother would watch them at night. Lamar would spend most of his time with them on the weekend when he was off work, and my mom gave us a break every now and then to have a date night. We had this setup going for at least five months. . . until Lamar called me into the living room to talk one evening after work; he said his company was shutting down indefinitely on the first of the year. He said he had known about it for some weeks, and that he tried looking for something else, not wanting to worry me. So far, however, he'd had no luck. I checked our savings, and it was only $3400. That wasn't going to last us more than a month with all the bills we had, and January was right around the corner. I was so upset with him for not telling me. We argued and argued about it until he rushed out of the room, slamming the door behind him.

After a few hours of blowing off steam, I told him I'd decided it was time for me to start looking for work again. He said, "Baby, just trust me. I'm going to find another job."

A month later, he did just that, but he took a big pay cut from the one he'd had before, so at that point, I had no other choice but to look for work to help out with the bills. Eventually, I got a job as an office clerk making $12.50 an hour.

I assumed the long hours Lamar and I spent at work took its toll on my mom, as she found a job as a nurse aide. Although I wanted to be happy for her, I now had to find daycare for the boys, which ended up being $350 a week. We were sinking in bills, and Lamar refused to take any money from my mom when she offered to help us out. So, when she got paid, she would stay gone until well after midnight, sometimes blowing all her money. We worked so much we hardly got to see each other, and all we ever talked about was bills. Once in a while, we'd have a quickie in the shower, but even those were rare.

* * *

Things got even worse. Lamar suffered a head injury that would put him out of work for a least three months. His workers' compensation wasn't that much, and already having dipped into the savings, we only had $1800 remaining. That wasn't how I'd imagined our marriage being. The stress was putting a strain on everything, so I had no other choice but to start making my mom pay some bills. She acted like she didn't mind, and she even picked up some extra hours to help pay for the boys' daycare expenses. A few weeks later, an accounting position opened up. I applied, and the interview went reasonably well, but in the back of my mind, I doubted myself because I was inexperienced. I couldn't use my prior internship as a reference, so all I could do was hope and pray that the manager would give me a try. I decided to keep everything about the job to myself until I found out if I had been selected or not; the last thing we needed was any more bad news.

As I anxiously waited for the weekend to fly by, I wasn't even paying attention to what was in front of me. Sunday night, Lamar made love to me so good. It was passionate, and he had never done it like that before. One thing that alarmed me was that he kept apologizing. It didn't sit well with my spirit afterward, so I tossed and turned all night. That morning, while I got ready for work, I asked him about it. He said he was sorry that I had to work so much. I could always tell when he was lying because he would rub his head twenty times in a minute, but I had to give him the benefit of the doubt and get to work early so that I could find out if I had been picked or not.

After I waited in the break room for a half-hour, the manager finally called me into his office and proceeded to scan my application. The complete silence made the news even more intense, and after about five minutes, he finally asked, "How would you like to become a paid intern for a few weeks, and afterward, start your new position with the company, making $57,000 a year?"

I couldn't believe it; what a roller coaster it had been. I'd gotten pregnant, had twins, been dropped from my previous internship, and lost one of my best friends, all in the same year. Who could have guessed that God had that blessing in store for me?

Chapter 5

Once I had finished filling out my paperwork, my boss let me leave early so I could celebrate. I was so excited that I couldn't wait to get home and tell Lamar the good news. I stopped off at the store to get some wine and ingredients for dinner. When I opened the trunk, I pushed all Lamar's work stuff aside to make room. As I did, a piece of paper fell out of his hardhat. I thought it strange, so I opened it to see what it was. I soon realized that it was a document from the clinic, containing test results. I rushed to put the rest of the bags into the trunk but took a minute to gather myself before opening the paper and examining it more closely.

I could feel my heart drop to my stomach. Lamar had tested positive for HIV. I sat there in total shock. On my way home, I wondered how he could have contracted it. Was he hooking up with an escort or something? What was it about me that made him want to be so disgusting and still lay down with me, knowing he was sick? I had been nothing but good to him. As the thoughts kept running through my head, I started feeling a rage like nothing I'd ever experienced. I cried and yelled to myself, contemplating how I was going to handle the situation when I got home. Minutes felt like hours, and I knew that the path that lay in front of me would be life-changing.

When I finally made it home, I sat in the driveway for a few minutes to get my mind somewhat together. Once I felt I had done so, I rushed upstairs to confront Lamar. I wasn't ready for what appeared in front of me. As I walked in, I saw Lamar on top of my mother in our bed with the door wide open. They were so into it that they didn't even realize I stood there. It dawned on me at that moment that she hadn't come to help me—she came to destroy me. As my eyes pierced with anger, I went down to the basement and got the .45 from the safe.

Once I made it upstairs, I blacked out. Once I finally realized what I had done, a cop tackled me.

While in that holding cell, waiting to be processed, I knew my life had changed just that quickly. A few days later, I received a court-appointed lawyer to handle my case. I was fighting both a murder and an attempted murder charge.

The prosecutors did their job well in making me sound like a monster. Since Lamar died, my lawyer made a plea for temporary insanity since I did catch him in the act with my mother, but that didn't do any good. The judge only dropped the attempted murder down to an aggravated assault since the other shot had only hit my mother in the shoulder. The verdict had been made: I was found guilty and sentenced eighteen years to life. I stood there in disbelief. Everything I had worked so hard for was gone. I would never know what it was like to be a successful accountant or see my kids grow up.

After years in solitary confinement on antidepressants, today, I'm a cook in the kitchen and help tutor other inmates to get their GED. I call my uncle Troy from time to time to put money on my books and give me updates about the boys since he has full custody of them now.

As for my mom, she moved back to Tennessee. She wrote me a letter not too long ago, mocking me about being stuck in prison. What really stood out in the letter was this: "How does it feel to lose everything, like I did when I had you?" She also detailed how many times she and Lamar had sex. Apparently, he'd been giving her money from our savings to keep her quiet. She'd given him that virus to torture me. How could such evil exist?

* * *

As I lie on this hard mat day after day, I think to myself, "What if Kelsie and I had just ridden off into the sunset together and been on some Morgan Freeman Bucket list, living life to the fullest until we were old and gray?" Instead, I'm here, and she's in the ground—all from thinking we loved the very person that would be our undoing. It's one thing, at least, that I've learned about life: you have to watch the ones who say they love you because they might just be detrimental to you.

** The End **

www.ingramcontent.com/pod-product-compliance
Lightning Source LLC
Chambersburg PA
CBHW070224180726
47999CB00017B/2311